Richard Levinge

A Day with the Brookside Harriers at Brighton

SALZWASSER
VERLAG

Richard Levinge

A Day with the Brookside Harriers at Brighton

Reprint of the original, first published in 1859.

1st Edition 2022 | ISBN: 978-3-37513-090-9

Verlag (Publisher): Salzwasser Verlag GmbH, Zeilweg 44, 60439 Frankfurt, Deutschland
Vertretungsberechtigt (Authorized to represent): E. Roepke, Zeilweg 44, 60439 Frankfurt, Deutschland
Druck (Print): Books on Demand GmbH, In de Tarpen 42, 22848 Norderstedt, Deutschland

A DAY

WITH THE BROOKSIDE HARRIERS

AT BRIGHTON.

A DAY

WITH THE BROOKSIDE HARRIERS

AT BRIGHTON.

BY

SIR RICHARD LEVINGE, BART. M.P.

LONDON:

G. ROUTLEDGE & CO. FARRINGDON STREET;

NEW YORK: 18, BEEKMAN STREET.

1858.

A Day with the Brookside Harriers

AT BRIGHTON.

—◇—

Behind she hears the hunters' cries,
And from the deep-mouth'd thunder flies;
She starts, she stops, she pants for breath,
She hears the near approach of death;
She doubles to mislead the hound,
And measures back her mazy ground.

A YARMOUTH bloater, which had been well soaked, an indifferent cup of tea—Brighton water is not famous for tea-making — very fresh prawns, and a fair share of marmalade, having been discussed with a sea-side appetite, I mounted my horse, Diachylum, one very foggy morning in the last week in November, to take a ride and lionize Brighton.

The beauty of Brighton, says one of its *habitués* and admirers, is, that we are clear of fogs when the London world is enveloped in the pea-soup raddle sort of medium, and, to do Brighton justice, it certainly gets off easier in this respect than most places I know; but this was not the case on the morning in question.

"Where shall I go?" said I to myself, half soliloquizing aloud. I remember to have heard that Jack Musters, the first of sportsmen, had said that when Leicestershire failed, he would go to Brighton and hunt there with the harriers; because hares run straight upon those downs, and like foxes!

"Sir," said Mr. Walton's foreman of the stables, where Diachylum lodged, "'the Brookside' are at Telscombe Tye to-day.

Go and have a look at them; it's only a
matter of five miles or so — it is better
than riding along our muddy streets this
foggy morning!"

But here again, to say a good word for old
Brighton—in no town I know of do the
trottoirs, at any rate, dry up so soon, being
generally made of brick, and kept scrupulously
clean; and if the great luminary will but
smile upon them, the most delicate of ladies,
in the very thinnest possible of *chaussures*,
and in the most splendid of dresses, may walk
along the Brighton *trottoirs* without the chance
of either being *abîmé*-d.

"But where is Telscombe Tye?"

"Go right along the cliff, sir, past Kemp
Town, and keep straight on; you will soon
find that you are not alone. Cannot mistake
the way, sir. They meet at eleven o'clock.
If you are late you will easily find them; get

on the top of a hill, and you will be sure to see them."

"But what about the fog?"

"Oh, I think that will clear off. But you will have to mind them downs, for it's very easy to get lost on 'em; it's a wery wild place, is them downs. I've heard tell of gentlemen as has not know'd the way back, and been a roaming about all night, and never see'd a soul to show them the way; and I heard tell that the whole pack once ran clean away from every one, huntsmen and all, and never were heard of until the next week!"

"Well, I will go at any rate, fog or no fog, and take my chance."

On turning out of one of those feeders that debouch at right angles upon the Esplanade, and down which the wind as well as flies can descend at a marvellous pace, I came upon a crowd craning over a chasm where some twenty or five-and-twenty feet of iron railing should have stood, but which had been carried away the night before. The smartest carriage in Brighton save one,—high-stepping dapple-grey horses, London coachman, powdered footman, bearskin hammer-cloth, gilt paws, and all, had been precipitated into Lady ———'s garden — an enclosed place some six or eight feet below the level of the roadway!

" How did it happen ? " said I to a coachman-like-looking fellow—" a horsey-looking gent," as *Punch* would designate him—in a fustian undress, with a short pipe in his mouth.

" Why, you see, sir, they was a driving quietly home—quite quietly like, after putting the missus down for dinner—and never seed that they had come to the end of Brunswick Terrace. The pole first caught the top cross-

bar of the railings, when down they went;
the horses they followed, came on their knees,
and dragged the carriage after them; the
coachman was shot right over their 'eads,
and the footman he was chucked clean over
them all."

"Were any of them hurt? Was the coachman screwed?"

"Screwed, sir! Lor' bles yer! no, sir—
sober as I am sir—saw it all happen myself;
nothing was the worse of it; they got the
carriage up again on planks,—no one was
hurt."

However, happen as it might, it was an
extraordinary escape, and I left that crowd
looking over the *débris* of iron railings,
smashed chrysanthemums, and mangled turf,
to be followed by others, day and night, until
all Brighton had stared at the place where a
carriage and pair, in spite of the iron notice,

"No thoroughfare," * had made a short cut from Hove into Brighton!

Leaving the mangled remains of the garden, I followed the Esplanade. The morning was frightfully cold, and the air being colder than the water, made the briny element smoke again, and a thick mist, independent of the fog was drifted to seaward by the north-east wind. I had never before witnessed this phenomenon in England, but frequently on the coasts of North America, where it is called by the "blue noses" of New Brunswick "The Barber."

All the army of bathing-machines were hauled up high and dry, as the sailors say, on the beach, bathing supposed to be over on the first of November—but one—one of Mary Hugget's, No. 112 (I like to be par-

* These iron railings are the boundary between the parishes of Hove and Brighton.

ticular about figures) ; that was launched,
and from it, at the extremity of a long rope,
was a female form. I could distinctly dis-
tinguish a profusion of the reddest possible
hair, as it flopped up and down.

Titian, Paul, Palma, old and young, Luini,
Gaudenzio Ferrari, and Raphael himself depicted Venuses, fine ladies, and Magdalenes,
with *capelli rossi;* and on talking the matter
over only yesterday with one who cut my
hair, and ought to be a good authority, if
the amount of his practice be any criterion,
exclaimed, "Red hair, sir—there is a great
feeling about red hair; but for my part, sir,
I consider it a vulgar prejudice, for the
ladies as have it in general has skins like
alley-blast-her ! "

I thought to myself, the fair object at the
extremity of Mrs. Hugget's line may not
have a skin, but certainly must have a frame,

of alley-blast-her to encounter this Brighton Barber!

So I left this mermaid

"A bobbing around, around,"

to encounter strings of the rising generation of both sexes walking very fast and very much out of step, on either side of the way.

The luxurious Bedford—prince of hotels— a string of flies, donkeys, and chairs—then the Flagstaff, its six guns and its warlike accompaniments; but they are to come away, and the Esplanade is to be carried straight on—a great improvement, by the way, and the sooner it is accomplished the better, then Mutton's, with its huge bowl (cracked), in which stewed pears swim, surrounded by little notices—" Made Dishes," " Soups ready," " Dinners dressed," " Suppers supplied;" in the next window, "Erin go

Bragh" surmounting a harp; underneath
"Choice Poteen from the Emerald Isle,"
all on an elaborate ground of shamrocks!

At this I started, it being a fine of one
hundred pounds to have a drop of poteen in
any one's possession in old Ireland; but as
I saw a coast-guard look-out not twenty
yards distant, I concluded it was all right
in Brighton.

Booty's circular window and circulating
library to boot, bonnet shops, pebbles and
jet, Childe's toy-shop, gay chessmen, back-
gammon-boards, and such loves of baskets!
Flies, chairs, donkey-carts, and a man with a
crimped hat upon his head with the Union
Jack emblazoned on it; another in his hand,
which he explains to you (if you will pay him
for it), changes into many forms, amongst
others a sentry-box in St. James's Park, or
a lady's fan!

Then the " Old Ship "—somehow or another
I like the look of the Old Ship—it gives the
idea of some fun and jovial souls with which it
was acquainted in days gone by. Mazes of
nets and a pile of fresh herrings just decanted
from a fishing-smack—all alive, oh!—and a
very good smell of pitch and tar—wholesome,
good smell, that tar—I like it! Then gay,
glittering Silvani's, where one longs to ruin
oneself; everything in the best of taste, from
a pen-wiper to the porcelains of Dresden,
Carpo di Monti, and Sèvres—*some* of it old!
But the taste for old china is quite as dangerous in its way, for those who are not
thoroughly acquainted with the present sys-
tem of repainting, as that for the old masters.

It is said the old Sèvres porcelain may be
known by the evenness of the glaze continued
over the piece, the absence of which to the
practised eye would denote that the medallions

of flowers, landscapes, or figures had been re-
painted. I am not speaking of the cross L.'s,
or the little hole often bored through the rim
of the piece underneath, of course they can
easily be made.

Trays full of charms, such as the Italian
ladies wear to keep off the " evil eye," or
their lovers, if they do not find a sufficient
confidence in themselves or in their prayers;
but theirs are generally of coral—beautiful
coral—these at Brighton are of all metals,
and no doubt are, in their way, quite as
effectual. Strange mixture! there are drums,
pistols, and cannons to keep off the officers;
but,—oh! perversity of female nature! a
slipper to attract them, an opera-glass to look
at them, a fish to catch them, a steam-engine
to run away with them, and a cage to hold
them!

Punchinello, a compass, a fan, an arm-chair,

and a boot-jack for the million; a tortoise and a mummy for the slow ones; a freemason's square and compass. But that will never reveal the secret to them.

A very old lady indeed is tottering along in a flat hat and a wonderful catskin tippet, meant to do duty for ermine, and a very young lady indeed,—the prettiest girl in Brighton, or perhaps anywhere else, with the most elastic of figures and the neatest possible feet and ankles, passing under a ladder; she does not know her danger. She will not be married this year at any rate, but six weeks will bring it to an end, and should these pages meet her eye, she may learn experience in the next year?*

Brill's Swimming-Bath, in which I hope to

---

* Probably she has; for since scribbling my *bagatelle*, I have learnt that the young lady in question is about to be united to a Kentish baronet, whom we all must envy.

B

have a plunge on my return; then the Pavilion—the *ci-devant* but not sea-side abode of royalty. By the bye, a quaint old print hangs up in the entrance-hall to Creke's Baths, and the porter there will act as cicerone, and point out the worthies and unworthies of that day, as they appear on the Old Steyne, then the New Steyne. The Duke of Queensbury and the Prince of Wales on horseback, accompanied by Colonel Leigh. To the right the Chain Pier, but I cannot see the end of it, the fog is so thick; a dangerous promenade, I should think, that must be now-a-days for the ladies, when a whisk of rude Boreas may reverse a steel petticoat, and the fair wearer may suddenly find herself garotted, but not robbed!

The Cliff is now ascended—its pretty, gay-looking houses—" Clarence Mansion," with its two lofty bay windows of plate-glass and bright green *jalousies*. Were I to have a house in Brighton, I should, judging by external appearances, like to have " Clarence Mansion." Further on is the house where Canning lived ; " the Bristol," with its three bows; then a horseman in long boots—like Rice's, but not nearly so neat—then the Duke of Devonshire's fresh-painted and gay-looking corner ; Lewis-crescent obscured by a labyrinth of tamarisk-quaint-looking stuff—tamarisk is said to be the only plant that will flourish in these parts, exposed to the sea-breeze, but it is not evergreen—and then comes Arundel-terrace ; the last Bath-chair; and—we are out of Brighton !

Straight along the cliffs, as Mr. Walton's foreman had told me, until I came to the turnpike, where I am asked for " Tuppence !"

All the turnpikes about Brighton are " tuppence !" When, in these days of railway, is this remnant of barbarism to cease ?

More horsemen now pass, and one lady.
Her horse is going at that indescribable pace
between a walk and a trot, but neither the one
nor the other. " It's a rack," says the Ameri-
can reader; " a market trot—butter and eggs,"
says my English reader. " Stuff!" says the
horseman; " the animal only wants holding
together!"

This was evidently the case, but its fair
freight has no idea of doing it; she has out-
distanced her master and party. She is sitting
across her horse, and shows a good deal of the
fog between her habit and the saddle, and does
so at regular periods! She has a very pretty
hand, though not a good one on a horse; her
waist is long—but not too long—her habit
does not fit: it is evidently hired with the
horse for the day's hunting. Her hair is
lovely, and is enclosed in a net studded with
little silver beads, which sparkled like dew-

drops in the fog as it appeared from under the coquettish little hat, well put on, with its scarlet feather. This and the habit, I thought, were faulty; and as I pass her, I can see a most elaborate arrangement of *crève-cœurs!* A chain of at least three are arranged in front of the tip of what must be a tiny little ear. Her profile is decidedly good; but I cannot imagine how the *crève-cœurs* stand the fog, damp weather being supposed to be fatal to curls; but probably the bandoline is *assez forte;* it cannot be mere sugar and water, it must be positive glue. *She* looks like mischief and going, but as the eye wanders downwards to her horse's fore-legs, they are, as the Yankee would say, " a caution !"

She is followed by another lady, a hobble-dehoy, on a hard-pulling roan, and a riding-master. The plot thickens, but the mist evidently thins; still the fog hangs gray and dense over the sea—a leaden-like weight upon it, making one giddy to look over those cliffs upon—nothing.

An effigy of a nondescript vessel looms through the haze, but no ship can be there, surely—the roar of the ocean is two hundred feet below; it looks to be cutter-rigged; it is neared, and turns out to be a coastguard station, having a mast, a topmast, and yard-arm rigged in front of it; from the topmast-head streams a pennant, and from the yard-arm a small red ensign. The whole looked neat and natty, as all government things of the sort do, standing in a small garden, with gravel walks, enclosed by a sprucely-trimmed hedge of tamarisk.—The number of these stations hereabouts is legion. What an expense to the country! Free-trade, indeed! why not free-trade in wine and oil as well as in corn?

Rottendean is passed, and I sidle on to the

green sward at the side of the road between it
and the yawning cliffs. The perfection of turf
to gallop over is on these downs, to be com-
pared only to that on the Curragh of Kildare;
so light, so corky; away I go, on, on over the
springy turf. Hurrah! the fog is lifting,
drifting away! The effect is grand; a bright,
light spot, brightening all the while, marks
where the sun means to make his appearance;
this completes the agreeable sensations the
canter had excited.

It will clear at twelve.

I then overtook a man who wore the
Queen's livery—a blue jacket, brass buttons,
and a nautical-looking cap; a long telescope is
under his arm, he has a peculiar walk, as
indeed they have in all professions—whether
the soldier, the sailor, the *flâneur*, the clod, or
the coastguardsman: this man was one of the
latter very expensive articles.

"Good-day."

"Good-day, sir."

"What is the weather going to do?"

"It will clear directly, sir; it's lifting to seaward, a certain sign that it will."

"What are those little heaps of white chalk placed for at such regular intervals as far as I can see?"

"They are to guide us as we walk along by night; if it was not for them, we could easily walk over the cliff."

"Do you often catch fellows smuggling?"

"Oh dear, no, sir. *Never*, sir; not in my time, sir? A long time ago I've heerd tell they did such things."

Another steep hill descended, and at the bottom another coastguard station is passed. This one appeared like a small village. The mist was all this time clearing off. To the right the broad sea, sulky and swollen, began to show signs of life here and there, and a sail was to be seen on the smoky horizon. To the left were the downs, dotted with clumps of gorse, and here and there were white scores of chalk; flies, phaetons, a basket-carriage on the road, more horsemen, and even horsewomen, in the valley and along the hill-tops.

On the far side of the hill is Telscomb Tye. But I was late; the music of the hounds and the horn can be heard. They are coming my way; a number of horses' heads appear on the hill-top. Another moment, huntsmen, horses, and hounds, men and all, are in view, going at a devil of a rate!

To my mind "The Brookside Harriers" are the prettiest pack of hounds I ever saw; they are so even in height, so prettily marked, and such good colours—all except one, a yellow dog, and I would draft him—he is too fast for the rest.

They are hunted admirably by Saxelby.

In his green coat and broad-brimmed hat, he looks, as he is, the right man in the right place; and though I am no lover of hare-hunting, I liked this turn-out.

The hares on these wild hills run straight—whether from being constantly hunted or not I cannot say, but they *do*—and, what is still more extraordinary, will go to ground like a fox! The poor thing they were following went for three or four miles nearly straight, but was eventually mobbed in a patch of turnips. This went against the grain—at least *with* me!

Hunting here reminded me more of that on the Campagna, near Rome, than of any other place or country I know. Here and there, too, a shepherd, leaning on his long staff in the distance, might easily be mistaken for a Roman *pastore*, and brought to my recollection a day

I had there some years ago, when Borghese
had the hounds—a tolerably good specimen of
a scratch-pack in the fullest sense of the word;
for when running at a pace known as "breast
high," a couple or three of the leading hounds
all of a sudden stopped dead short! There
were no holes that I could see, or any sort of
place for a fox to have disappeared in. After
quite a scene had been enacted, they were
eventually whipped off.

"What is it?" I said—"what did they
come to fault about?"

The reply from my Italian friend, in *sotto
voce,* was: "They are truffle dogs! they found
truffles! and when they find them they navare
will leave them. They will go scratch, scratch;
they like them, evair so much better as one
fox."

There are no fences on these downs, but
some riding is required. The hills are very

steep, very slippery at times, and there are
treacherous cart-tracks overgrown, which re-
quire a little management and quartering, as
do "the ridge and furrow," well known to
those who have ridden over high Leicestershire.

The sketch in *Punch* of Mr. Briggs is not
much exaggerated, where he is depicted as en-
joying a day with the Brighton harriers, when
having ascended one hill just to descend
another as steep, Montaigne Russe-like, has
to put on steam enough to force himself up
the third! It is perfectly astonishing to the
uninitiated how some of the horses, with the
sort of fore-legs they possess, can carry their
riders down such precipices; yet they do, poor
things; and many of them have a turn on the
Esplanade in the afternoon!

Well—I joined the chase, and a right good
pace did these little hounds go. " No tailing,"

to use a fox-hunter's hackneyed expression;
you might " cover them with a sheet."

During the ardour of the chase, and as I was
nearing the top of one of these descents, all at
once rush came by me, his nose high in air, a
thorough-bred horse, going at the rate of fifty
miles an hour, bearing its fair freight, who, at
a glance, I recognized to be her of the elbows
and the spangled net, from which her hair at
one side was streaming; but the same glance
enabled me to see that the arrangement of
crève-cœurs still stood ! In her wake came the
hobbledehoy on the roaring roan, and close
alongside of the Amazon raced the riding-
master, hanging on her quarter (as the sailors
would say), and luckily on her bridle too—just
in time to force her horse's head round as she
was going to charge down the precipice, and
away he went instead in a contrary direction.
The roan followed suit—not so its rider; the

young gentleman made very short work of it—
he simply threw himself off !

Having had a capital gallop, I turned my
horse's head in the direction of Brighton, and
left the Brookside harriers to look for another
hare. Englishmen in general have a strong
prejudice against hare-hunting, in which I have
been always inclined to join. " There is something grand," they say, " in hunting the wild
fox ;"—that is an English fox-hunter's opinion.

What a Frenchman's is, we once heard too ;
" You English are one extraordinary people ;
you have, for example, your *chasse au renard*—
your fox-hunting, as you call it; you ride all
one long day after a great many dogs and one
stinking animal, and when you have catch him
at last, you can neyvere eat him !"

" Mais revenons à nos moutons," as the
French would say.

I left the Brookside harriers, well pleased

with the capital sport they had shown, and quite impressed with the fact that hare-hunting on these downs, whatever it might be elsewhere, was a very good pastime. No end of amusement in one shape or the other is afforded to the looker-on, who gets a good gallop in the freshest possible air and over the most delightful turf, and can reach Brighton in good time to wash, dress, and flirt.

The day is now gloriously fine and the sun shines. My horse starts at the streaky shadows made by the arms of a windmill. Irish horses are not accustomed to windmills.

The tide is out, and men are shrimping; a couple of blue crows are pluming themselves on the cliff, and a couple more coast-guard stations are passed which I had not remarked on my way out in the morning.

The very face of Brighton is changed as I re-enter it and encounter crowds on horseback.

Riding-masters, surrounded and followed by squadrons of ladies; flies, donkeys, goats, chairs and perambulators, pedestrians in various de‑ grees of fanciful morning costume, two or three bands, organ-grinders, a monkey mounted on a greyhound, armed *cap à pied,* Lewis's Marion‑ ettes, brandy-balls, and a long horn heralding forth the birth of the *Brighton Gazette* of the day, a small boy or two, " *Heralds* and *Stars,* only a penny !" and jolly, good-humoured old Punch, with his own peculiar scream.

I love old Punch, and am never tired of him, be he where he may. This one was at the corner of West Street—undeniably good. But the people will all go in to luncheon soon, and so shall I, after I have been to Brill's Baths ! Nothing can be better than all the arrange‑ ments; its ante-room, with newspapers, the list of the hounds, and the telegraphic des‑ patches. In the huge cauldron of parboiled sea-water, five or six men are at the same time to be seen swimming, and the head of one who cannot swim.

I asked if fresh water was supplied. "Oh yes, sir—pumped up every morning from the sea." "And can one come at any time?" "Yes; any hour from eight in the morning until ten at night."

I thought that the water might be fresh probably in the morning, but the company certainly was numerous.

"Do the schools ever come here?" "Yes, many of them."

The bowl in Mutton's window, and the pears swimming in it, came into my head! I did not fancy washing for the million, and retired to the Brunswick Baths, thinking that in *this* case, at all events, solitude was the best company. Here I saw the water rush into the marble basin fresh and sparkling.

Having discussed a dozen and a half of oysters, with their proportionate quantity of most delicious brown bread-and-butter, I went to the window. "The barber," or sea-fog of the morning had mystified the outward surface, and elongated the objects seen through the glass in one direction, while in the other a reverse effect was visible. I cannot see very plainly into the bay window opposite, but I do think I can discover a lady amusing herself with an opera-glass—a double barrelled one.

What *is* she looking at?

The sea, of course, for there is nothing else to be seen—from my side at any rate—down the opening at the end of the street; but the sea is smooth and tranquil, not a ruffle upon its bright surface, not a vessel even.

She is leaning back. I cannot see her face, only her taper little fingers as she directs the glasses. She has some rings, but the jewellery

does not look first-rate. It is bad, decidedly;
probably a forget-me-not, or something after
that fashion, on an onyx stone; but she has a
plain one on the fourth finger of her left hand,
so she may be a widow.

She has changed her position a little, but I
cannot see her face, *that* is still behind the
curtain; there is a fairy foot, and a very mis-
chievous-looking slipper with a bow upon it,
as it peeps from under a bit of lace-looking
work, and a red petticoat, of course; *ce n'est
pas mal*, but in altering her position she has
also brought her glasses to bear in another
direction—a little more to the right. I fancy
she has been at work, for at the same time she
balances a ball of white cotton on the cross-
bar of the middle window of the bay, where it
steadies itself. I can see nothing, so I con-
clude the sea—the boundless sea—is still the
object of attraction.

I turned from the window to light a cigar, but the fire had gone out, and my fuzees were damp, and I was some time bungling before I could get my cigar a-going, when a knock at the opposite door attracted my attention.

I cannot tell *why*, but I looked instinctively first at the bay-window where the glasses had disappeared, and I could just catch through the gloom a glimpse of a retiring form as it disappeared in the depth of obscurity. A man is standing at the door. I cannot see his face for his whiskers; he looks all hair and teeth, like a ratcatcher's dog. A spruce-looking maid opens the door, and is sent up, no doubt, to know if the inmates are at home. Quick as lightning, something which glistened, and looked very like a key, is tried in the lock. It fits, evidently—*if* it be a key. His hand turned first upwards and then back again, but the movement was so rapidly made, and the windows so obscured, as I have before said, that it might be a pencil-case which he returned—with an evident look of satisfaction—so quietly to his waistcoat pocket —probably intending to write his address or something on the card, which he now holds in his hand, but which he goes away without even giving to the maid.

He could not have reached the corner, but still was out of my sight before she was at the window again; and this time I see her profile. *Corpo di Bacco !* she is lovely—so piquante ! a straight nose, slightly *retroussé*, a full under lip, —but what *is* she at ? What strange manœuvering is going on? She is arranging more balls of white cotton on the bow of the window — one, two, three, four, five, six, seven—and the one placed there in the first instance, that makes eight. I looked at my watch, shook the ashes off my cigar, took my hat and gloves, and returned once more to the Esplanade.

The evening is lovely, and the inhabitants of Brighton are pouring out from every house and street like bees from a hive, and the buzz along the Esplanade increases, and is even heard above the rumbling of the carriages or the murmuring of the retiring tide. What a sight it was!—all pleasure-seekers—at least apparently so; no poverty appears here—no rags, at any rate; but the back slums of Brighton might tell a different tale. No beggars, save the few professionals, dare to follow the rich crowd.

A propos of professional beggars, I recollect a good story told of one of this race, a well-known character, one Maggy, in a town in Ireland. The poor-house had just been completed, to their horror. One of the great un-

paid guardians, strutting in all the importance
and dignity of his appointment, to which he
had that day been elected, accosted Maggy :—
" Well, Maggy, how are you ?   Have you seen
the fine house we have built for you ?"   " Oh,
your honour! long life to you!   Remember
your poor ould widders, and give me a little
sixpence this morning to break my fast !"
"Oh! no, Maggy; no more begging allowed
now ! go to the poor-house, and *I* will take
care that you are admitted."   " Is it to *that*
place you would send me, your honour?   I go
to the poor-house *to be washed !—to be washed
like a baby !   I'd die first !*"

The crowd along the Esplanade seemed a
motley one, and to be composed of collections
from Hyde Park of a Sunday, and from Rotten
Row and the Drive on a week-day.   Here all
amalgamated.   Some few friends, and many
faces one had often seen—*somewhere ;* and how

smartly dressed are the ladies, and how well
chaussé-d !

There is something mischievous about those
well-fitting Balmoral boots, so nicely and
pliantly laced up, and the old custom revived
of looping up the dresses, the parti-coloured
petticoats sufficiently distended to show their
well-turned ankles; but this is a sea-side
privilege.

An open barouche dashes by—a dark-
blue body with light-blue wheels, and black
horses—such steppers! and such a love of
a crimson bonnet! Amongst the pedestrians, Captain O'Grady, a regular watering-
place half-pay lady-killer, of a florid com-
plexion, rather given to corpulency, but
very upright—in his appearance —whiskers
which, were they combed out to their full
extent, must have been enormous, but now
curled up tight with an instrument—derived

from some Greek word tortured into—called
a bostrokizon!

I thought I had seen some very like them
lately. It was only a passing thought as I
scanned the rest of his elaborate but mistaken
toilet, the *beau idéal* of what ladies'-maids
would call a very handsome man—and—he
knew it too! His coat was an evening one,
which hardly met across the chest; but that
was of no consequence, for he was evidently
addicted to a display of jewellery, and a meet-
ing was effected by means of a couple of agate
buttons—Brighton pebbles—connected by a
short gold cable, which strained the coat
together, and from just below this connection,
and hung up to his waistcoat by a gold shepherd's-looking hook, dangled an enormous
bunch of coral charms, patent-leather boots,
and a cane with a verde antique top to switch
them with! He was heard to say that he never

saw such illegant females in his life, that
Carrick-on-Shannon was a joke to Brighton,
and that no man in his senses could stand
them, with their neat little heads, the darlings,
and their little boots, and those petticoats!
Did you ever see anything so gaudy? By the
powers, if they were only to be walking along
the banks of the Shannon instead of the
Esplanade, why, the very salmon themselves
would rise at them!

As I neared the Flagstaff, and crossed with
the crowd, I came upon Mason's Repository
of Arts, and found myself—by permission of
somebody—confronted with " General Have-
lock ;" a little lower down in the morning
I had seen a crowd staring at " What o'clock
it was at Lucknow "—two long rival prints;
the " Duke on the Field of Waterloo," by
Landseer; and the " Horse Fair," by Rosa
Bonheur — both beautiful engravings. It

would be treason to say I liked the latter
the best; long as it was, it did not appear,
at any rate, so long as the other.

The Brighton Talbotype Gallery, in large
letters above that of the Repository of Arts,
induced me to make inquiries, and to find my
way through the shop and up a couple of
flights of steps, until I was brought up by the
formidable machine of Messrs. Henna and
Kent, where there were numerous duplicate
likenesses of the Brighton and other swells,
amongst them one of O'Grady in his coral
charms—most faithfully depicted. The thought
at once struck me that I would submit to the
operation myself, in case any lady should fancy
herself in love with the author of "A Day
with the Brookside Harriers."

Talk of the face pulled when at a dentist's,
the same cold thrill runs up the spine as our
head is leaned—quietly to be sure—against

the iron support, to "steady it just for the moment." They say it is better to look rather away than towards the instrument; but look as you may, when the glass upon which the likeness is taken has had its bath in the *acid*, you will come out excessively cross, and so did I; therefore, I warn my lady friend that I have not been done justice to!

For dinner a sea-side appetite again. Among other things stewed pears made their appearance; they were coarse and rough, and the syrup very thin. Could they have been in company in the morning with those in the cracked bowl at Mutton's? No other disagreements as to the repast, save the chestnuts at desert; they were not sufficiently roasted! had not been nicked, or probably not boiled enough before the roasting process; at any rate, the brusiata was not correct, and even a red-hot shovel did not mend matters. So, lighting another cigar—my second this day—I left for the Esplanade once more, *en route* to the theatre. Some one lets himself in at the opposite door with a latch key, a shadow of a large pair of whiskers disappears along the glazed passage-papered walls, and the door closes gently. The eight balls of cotton! And it is now eight o'clock—so Captain O'Grady I smell a rat!

But then the state of my windows in the *morning*—it may be a mistake after all.

" *Honi soit qui mal y pense.*"

The moon is up, and a great deal of company is on the Esplanade—not exactly the same sort of company as were there three hours ago—but still there were numbers of red petticoats, as well as I could see, and a great many cigars were alight.

" The devil's in the moon," I heard one man exclaim, as he passed. No doubt he was quoting aloud from Byron.

The morals of Brighton must be quite safe, thanks to the abundance of charms to be had at Silvani's, and numerous other shops for their retail.

A very prim old maid of the blue-stocking school, who had no faith in these charms, once expressed her horror of the state of society in general, and London in particular, to a very fast but very fashionable lady, not quite so prim as herself.

" Yes," was the reply of the fast lady, who had a good many charms of her own (as well as of coral), " my husband who is in the House, and takes an interest in the sort of thing, tells me the statistics point to 60,000, and that, you know, my dear, does not include the amateurs !"

"A beggarly account of empty boxes," indeed, that theatre presented—it is not supported by the *élite* of Brighton, that is evident; there were not half-a-dozen people in what is called the "dress circle;" but I passed the remainder of the evening pleasantly enough with "Jack Shepherd," which was very well done. Lit another cigar (my third and last), but they were small and very good ones— Dash's king's regalias—and thus concluded, to me, at least, a very pleasant day in jolly, gay Brighton. I went to bed and slept like a top, and if the reader be not bored by the description, we may meet elsewhere some other day.

COX AND WYMAN, PRINTERS, GREAT QUEEN STREET, LONDON.